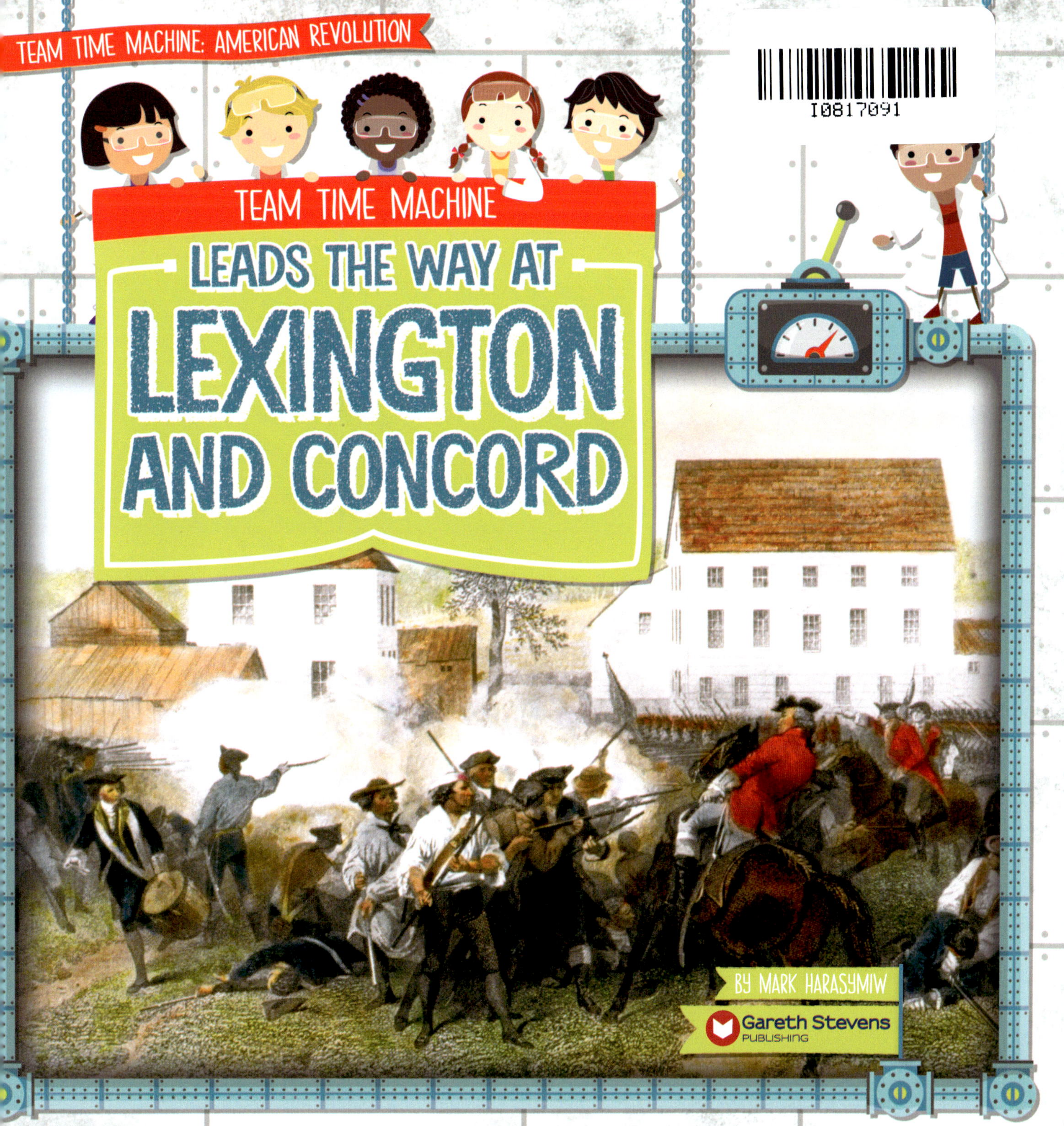
TEAM TIME MACHINE: AMERICAN REVOLUTION
TEAM TIME MACHINE
LEADS THE WAY AT
LEXINGTON
AND CONCORD
BY MARK HARASYMIW
Gareth Stevens
PUBLISHING
I0817091

Please visit our website, www.garethstevens.com. For a free color catalog of all our high-quality books, call toll free 1-800-542-2595 or fax 1-877-542-2596.

Library of Congress Cataloging-in-Publication Data

Names: Harasymiw, Mark, author.

Title: Team time machine leads the way at Lexington and Concord / Mark Harasymiw.
Description: New York : Gareth Stevens Publishing, [2020] | Summary: "The Team Time Machine kids are going back in time to a famous moment in American history–when American colonists battled the British forces at Lexington and Concord. As riveted readers tag along, the time-traveling adventurers witness these Revolutionary War battles and the British march back to Boston, setting the stage for the revolution that created the United States. Historical images and fun fact boxes give budding historians an in-depth understanding of these significant events"–
Provided by publisher.
Identifiers: LCCN 2019021350 | ISBN 9781538246863 (paperback) | ISBN 9781538246887 (library binding) | ISBN 9781538246870
Subjects: LCSH: Lexington, Battle of, Lexington, Mass., 1775–Juvenile literature. | Concord, Battle of, Concord, Mass., 1775–Juvenile literature.
Classification: LCC E241.L6 H375 2020 | DDC 973.3/311-dc23
LC record available at https://lccn.loc.gov/2019021350

First Edition

Published in 2020 by
Gareth Stevens Publishing
111 East 14th Street, Suite 349
New York, NY 10003

Designer: Katelyn E. Reynolds
Editor: Therese Shea

Photo credits: Cover, p. 1, 23, 25 Bettmann/Getty Images; cover, pp. 1–24 (series characters) Lorelyn Medina/Shutterstock.com; cover, pp. 1–24 (time machine elements) Agor2012/Shutterstock.com; cover, pp. 1–24 (background texture) somen/Shutterstock.com; p. 5 Ed Vebell/Getty Images; p. 7 Yale Center for British Art, Paul Mellon Collection (http://collections.britishart.yale.edu/vufind/Record/1668328)/Hohum/Wikipedia.org; p. 9 MPI/Getty Images; p. 11 National Army Museum/(http://www.redcoat.org/history/smith.html)/Magicpiano/Wikipedia.org; pp. 13, 27 Hulton Archive/Getty Images; p. 15 Nigar Alizada/Shutterstock.com; p. 17 Interim Archives/Getty Images; p. 19 Fotosearch/Getty Images; p. 19 Map courtesy of National Park Service; p. 21 Breck P. Kent/Shutterstock.com; p. 29 De Agostini Picture Library/Getty Images.

Printed in the United States of America

CONTENTS

Chapter 1: Back to 1775 4
Chapter 2: The British Come to Lexington 8
Chapter 3: First Shots Fired 12
Chapter 4: The Searching of Concord 16
Chapter 5: Battle at North Bridge 22
Chapter 6: The Long March Back to Boston 24
Chapter 7: To the Time Machine! 28
Glossary 30
For More Information 31
Index 32

WORDS IN THE GLOSSARY APPEAR IN **BOLD** TYPE THE FIRST TIME THEY ARE USED IN THE TEXT.

CHAPTER 1: BACK TO 1775

One morning, Gaby, Zoe, and Will were talking about their many adventures. One had left them wanting to know more.

"Do you remember riding with Paul Revere when he warned the American colonists British soldiers were coming?" asked Gaby. "I wonder what happened after that!"

"We heard some of the first shots of the **American Revolution**, but we didn't get to see the battles," said Zoe.

"Did the **patriots** win their first fight against the **redcoats**?" asked Will.

"I know how to find out!" exclaimed Gaby. "To the library!"

MEET TEAM TIME MACHINE

TEAM TIME MACHINE IS A GROUP OF FRIENDS WHO FOUND A TIME MACHINE ONE DAY IN A VERY ODD LIBRARY. THEY DISCOVERED THAT BOOKS FROM THE LIBRARY COULD POWER THE MACHINE AND TRANSPORT THEM TO DIFFERENT PLACES AND TIMES. IN THIS ADVENTURE, GABY, ZOE, AND WILL WITNESS THE BATTLES AT LEXINGTON AND CONCORD!

GETTING EXCITED ABOUT HISTORY IS EASY WHEN YOU'RE PART OF TEAM TIME MACHINE. WHEN THEY WANTED TO LEARN ABOUT PAUL REVERE'S MIDNIGHT RIDE, THEY FOLLOWED HIM ON HORSEBACK!

At the Team Time Machine library, the kids began searching for the book that would start their journey to **colonial** Lexington and Concord. Zoe found one and slipped it into an opening in the machine. With a pull of the handle, they were off! After a shaky few moments, the machine read: "April 19, 1775."

"We've arrived on the right day," said Will. "I wonder if we're early enough to watch the British soldiers arrive."

"Be careful out there, team!" said Zoe. "A war is about to begin!"

GENERAL THOMAS GAGE SENT BRITISH SOLDIERS TO CONCORD, MASSACHUSETTS, TO CAPTURE **WEAPONS**, GUNPOWDER, AND OTHER MILITARY SUPPLIES. THE SOLDIERS HAD TO MARCH THROUGH LEXINGTON TO GET THERE.

CHAPTER 2: THE BRITISH COME TO LEXINGTON

Zoe, Gaby, and Will peered around the door of the library, which now looked like a colonial shop. They stepped into Lexington, Massachusetts. The sun was just starting to brighten the sky. The kids saw more than 70 men standing in a grassy field. The men held muskets, a kind of long gun.

"Who are those men? Why are they just standing around in the town green?" asked Will.

"I think they're the Lexington **militia**," answered Gaby. "They're waiting for the British soldiers to arrive."

CAPTAIN JOHN PARKER WAS THE LEADER OF THE COLONIAL MILITIA AT LEXINGTON. HE HAD FOUGHT FOR THE BRITISH IN THE **FRENCH AND INDIAN WAR**.

AMONG THE COLONIAL MILITIA WERE MINUTEMEN. THESE WERE MEN WHO PROMISED TO BE READY TO FIGHT "AT A MINUTE'S WARNING." THEY WERE THE FIRST TO A FIGHT.

Soon after, the kids heard the approach of marching British soldiers.

"Let's get closer to the militia to see what happens next," suggested Zoe.

"This is where the fighting begins!" warned Gaby. "Let's stay behind this stone wall so we don't get hurt." The kids watched about 800 British soldiers march into Lexington.

"There are so many!" exclaimed Will. "The colonists can't hope to fight them and win!" A militia leader ordered his men to disperse, or scatter, soon after the British arrived in Lexington.

A BRITISH OFFICER YELLED AT THE MILITIA STANDING ON LEXINGTON GREEN TO THROW DOWN THEIR WEAPONS. LIEUTENANT COLONEL FRANCIS SMITH, SHOWN HERE, WAS ONE OF THE BRITISH LEADERS THAT DAY.

CHAPTER 3: FIRST SHOTS FIRED

Just after the militia was ordered to leave, the kids heard a gunshot.

"Who fired?" asked Zoe, looking around. Before Gaby or Will could answer, the redcoats began firing at the patriots.

The kids ducked their heads and ran for the safety of a nearby building. They didn't look out until the firing stopped. When it finally did, the air was filled with smoke. As the smoke slowly cleared, Gaby, Zoe, and Will saw several militiamen on the ground.

NO ONE KNOWS WHO FIRED THE FIRST SHOT AT LEXINGTON THAT DAY. HISTORIANS STILL ARGUE ABOUT IT.

EIGHT MILITIAMEN WERE KILLED AT LEXINGTON, AND 10 MORE WERE WOUNDED. ONLY ONE BRITISH SOLDIER WAS WOUNDED.

Gaby, Zoe, and Will watched as the militia walked off the town green. The British left, too, marching toward Concord. The people of Lexington came out of their homes to help care for the wounded militiamen. The kids approached a young man who was carrying water to the men. He said his name was Simon.

"Who was the leader of the Lexington militia?" Zoe asked him.

"That was Captain John Parker," answered Simon. "He didn't want to fight, but I think the battle changed his mind. He looked angry."

CAPTAIN PARKER WOULDN'T LIVE MUCH LONGER. HE HAD **TUBERCULOSIS** AND WOULD DIE 5 MONTHS LATER, ON SEPTEMBER 17, 1775.

CHAPTER 4: THE SEARCHING OF CONCORD

The kids decided to follow the British soldiers to Concord. Simon asked to tag along. They arrived at the town around 8 a.m. The British soldiers were spreading out in groups. Their leaders were barking orders at them, pointing in different directions.

"It looks like the soldiers are searching for something," said Simon. "What could it be?"

Gaby answered, "They're looking for weapons and gunpowder that the colonists have hidden here."

Soon, they saw the British soldiers burning supplies they found.

THE BURNING PILES OF MILITARY SUPPLIES MADE THE MILITIAMEN OUTSIDE CONCORD THINK THE BRITISH WERE BURNING THE WHOLE TOWN DOWN!

THE BRITISH SOLDIERS DIDN'T FIND MANY OF THE MILITIA'S SUPPLIES IN CONCORD. MOST HAD BEEN MOVED WHEN THE COLONISTS HAD RECEIVED THE MESSAGE THAT THE BRITISH WERE COMING FOR THEM.

Simon spotted a group of about 200 British soldiers moving away from the main group and toward them! He told Gaby, Zoe and Will, "I think they're heading to the North Bridge. If they cross it, it's not too much farther to Barrett Farm where the militia keeps their weapons!"

Gaby said, "Let's cross the bridge before they do. We have to be careful—we don't want to get caught!"

The kids quickly moved north to the bridge and crossed the Concord River.

WHILE THE BRITISH SEARCHED CONCORD FOR ABOUT 4 HOURS, MORE AND MORE MILITIA WERE ARRIVING FROM AROUND THE AREA.

THE BRITISH MARCH TO LEXINGTON AND CONCORD

Barrett Farm
North Bridge
CONCORD
LEXINGTON
BRITISH ROUTE TO CONCORD
BOSTON
Concord River
Assabet River
Mystic Lakes
Mystic River
MYSTIC RIVER
Alewife Brook
Walden Pond
Flint Pond
Hobbs
Sudbury River
CHARLES RIVER
Back Bay

At the North Bridge, Simon said, "Let's go to the high ground on the other side. We'll be able to get a good view of the British movements from there."

As they climbed uphill, the kids came upon about 400 militiamen. The men were talking about the fires in Concord, which they thought were burning buildings. One of the militiamen shouted, "Will you let them burn the town down?" The militia decided to march into town to stop the British.

TODAY'S NORTH BRIDGE IS THE FIFTH ONE THAT'S BEEN BUILT THERE. THE NORTH BRIDGE FROM 1775 WAS TAKEN DOWN IN 1788.

CHAPTER 5: BATTLE AT NORTH BRIDGE

"We should stay up here for now. It's way too dangerous to follow the militia on their march toward the British," said Gaby.

Hundreds of patriots marched toward the North Bridge. The redcoats **retreated** across to the other side and waited. The leader of the militia, Colonel James Barrett, ordered his men not to fire on the British soldiers unless the British fired first.

The British did fire, killing two militiamen. The colonists fired back, killing several soldiers and wounding others.
The British moved back into town.

THE COLONISTS FIRING ON THE BRITISH AT NORTH BRIDGE IS SOMETIMES CALLED "THE SHOT HEARD ROUND THE WORLD."

CAPTAIN ISAAC DAVIS WAS ONE OF THE COLONISTS KILLED BY THE BRITISH AT THE NORTH BRIDGE.

After the smoke cleared from the fighting on the bridge, the children followed the militia into Concord. The British were leaving the town and marching down the road back to Lexington.

Simon said proudly, "After the battles today, patriots all over the countryside will believe they can stand up to the redcoats!"

"Let's follow the British soldiers—but not too closely!" said Will.

"I'll go back to Lexington with you," said Simon. "If there's to be a war, I need to prepare."

THE BRITISH SOLDIERS HAD TO MARCH ABOUT 18 MILES (29 KM) FROM CONCORD BACK TO BOSTON.

AS THE KIDS FOLLOWED THE BRITISH SOLDIERS BACK TO BOSTON, THEY SAW GROUPS OF MILITIA FIRING FROM BEHIND TREES, HOUSES, AND FENCES.

John Parker, the leader of the militia at Lexington, led his group of men in an **ambush** against the retreating British soldiers. Team Time Machine was careful to keep a lot of space between themselves and the fighting.

As they approached Boston, Zoe said, "I don't think the firing has stopped for more than 5 minutes since we left Concord!" The others agreed. It was like endless thunder.

The British controlled Boston. Once they reached that city, the soldiers were safe. It was now close to 8 p.m.

ACCORDING TO MANY SOURCES, BRITISH LOSSES FOR THE DAY WERE ABOUT 73 MEN KILLED AND 174 WOUNDED. THE COLONISTS LOST ABOUT 49 MEN WHILE 39 MORE WERE WOUNDED.

CHAPTER 7: TO THE TIME MACHINE!

"Today was called a **disaster** for the British. Without Paul Revere and others warning about the British plans, it could have been a disaster for the patriots!" said Gaby.

"What an adventure!" exclaimed Zoe. "We started in a battle in Lexington, went to another battle in Concord, and then marched back to Boston!"

"And now we have to march all the way back to the library in Lexington—and get home!" said Will.

"Or to the next adventure?" suggested Gaby. The team grinned at each other and started walking.

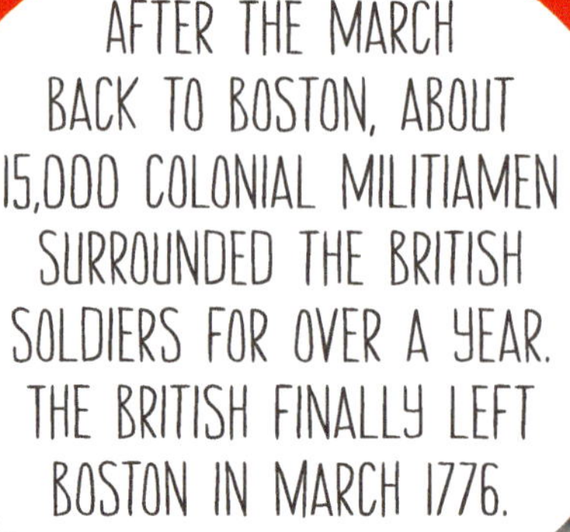

AT THE BATTLE OF BUNKER HILL IN JUNE 1775, THE BRITISH FORCES TRIED TO BREAK THE MILITIA'S **SIEGE** OF BOSTON. ALTHOUGH THE BRITISH WON THAT DAY, THE BATTLE WAS SO HARD THEY DIDN'T BREAK THE SIEGE.

GLOSSARY

ambush: a surprise attack

American Revolution: the war in which the colonies won their freedom from England

colonial: having to do with colonies, which are lands under the control of another country

disaster: an event that causes much suffering, loss, or harm

French and Indian War: a war between France and England fought in North America from 1754 to 1763

militia: a group of citizens who organize like soldiers in order to protect themselves

patriot: one who was on the side of the colonies during the American Revolution

rebel: one who fights to overthrow a government

redcoat: a name for a British soldier during the American Revolution

retreat: to move away from danger or attack

siege: the use of military to surround an area or building in order to capture it

tuberculosis: a serious illness that affects the lungs

weapon: something used to fight an enemy

FOR MORE INFORMATION

BOOKS

Haugen, Brenda. *The Split History of the Battles of Lexington and Concord: Patriot's Perspective.* North Mankato, MN: Compass Point Books, 2018.

Whitwell, Stephen. *The Battles of Lexington and Concord: First Shots of the American Revolution.* New York, NY: PowerKids Press, 2016.

WEBSITES

Battle at Lexington Green, 1775
www.eyewitnesstohistory.com/lexington2.htm
Read a report of the day's events from a British soldier's view.

Lexington and Concord
www.battlefields.org/learn/revolutionary-war/battles/lexington-and-concord
Find out more about the Battles of Lexington and Concord.

Three Men from Acton
www.battlefields.org/learn/articles/three-men-acton
Learn about the minutemen of Acton, Massachusetts.

INDEX

ambush 26

American Revolution 4

Barrett Farm 18, 19

Barrett, James 22

Battle of Bunker Hill 29

colonist 4, 10, 16, 17, 22, 23, 27

Concord River 18

Davis, Isaac 20, 23

French and Indian War 8

Gage, Thomas 7

Lexington Green 11

militia 8, 9, 10, 11, 12, 14, 16, 17, 18, 19, 20, 22, 24, 25, 26, 28, 29

minutemen 9

North Bridge 18, 19, 20, 21, 22, 23

Parker, John 8, 14, 15, 26

patriot 4, 12, 22, 24

rebel 26

redcoat 4, 12, 22, 24

Revere, Paul 4, 5, 28

"shot heard round the world" 22

siege 29

Smith, Francis 11, 18

tuberculosis 15

weapons 7, 11, 16, 18